The Boy Who Cried Shark

SHARK SCHOOL

The Boy Who Cried Shark

BY DAVY OCEAN
ILLUSTRATED BY AARON BLECHA

SCHOLASTIC INC.

WiTH THANKS TO PAUL EBBS

Originally published as *Harry Hammer: Shark Alert* in 2013 in Great Britain by Templar Publishing

ISBN 978-1-338-08714-7

12 11 10 9 8 7 6 5 4 3 2 1   16 17 18 19 20 21

Printed in China   68

This edition first printing, September 2016

Cover designed by Karin Paprocki
Interior designed by Mike Rosamilia
The text of this book was set in Write Demibd.

CHAPTER 1

Zoooooooooooooooooooooooooooom!

Out of my room . . .

Screeeeeeeeeeeeeeeeeeeeeech!

Down the stairs . . .

Ziiiiiiiiiiiiiiiiiiiiiiiiiiiiiiiiiiiiiiingg!

Into the hall . . .

YOOOOOOOOOOOOOOOOWLLLL!!!

"Sorry, Puddles!" I call back as I crash into our moth-eared catfish, sending him spinning out of control and bouncing into the wall. I don't stop to find out if he's all right. I must get to the jellyfishion before Mom and Dad!

It's Saturday night, and if I don't get there RIGHT NOW, they'll put on the news or some terrible sappy movie. They've been washing the dishes while I've been cleaning my room. There's always a rush to get to the den first after dinner, but tonight I *have* to get there first. So, instead of doing a total cleanup, I used my tail to sweep the mess under my bed. If Mom doesn't look too closely, I might just get away with it.

I come to the end of the hall, hook my dorsal on the doorframe, spin sideways (so my goofy hammery head doesn't get stuck in the door), and then—WHAM!—I'm in the den. Before Mom and Dad. YES!

Sailing around tail first, I slide into the finchair closest to the flat-screen jellyfishion and reach out with the flukes on my tail to flick the remote control off the coffee table and—

CLICK!

—down on the on button.

With a shiver and a fizz, the jellyfishion comes to life and I left-hammer the three button, just in time to see the judges for *The Shark Factor* being introduced. Pumping music blares and lasers burst across the stage, lighting the huge undersea set. The announcer, with his big, booming whale-size voice, waits for the pumping music to stop and then shouts out the names of the judges as they appear.

"Paddy!"

That's Paddy Snapper, the saltwater crocodile from Emerald Island. He slithers down the ramp on his yellow belly.

"Ellie!"

That's Ellie Electra, the smooth-bodied electric eel with ultra-shiny skin. She shimmies down the ramp and wraps herself around Paddy.

"Bobby!"

That's Bobby Barnacle, who is so tiny, he slides down the ramp under his own

personal magnifying glass so that everyone can see him.

"Marcus!"

And lastly, it's Marcus Sea-cow, wearing his trademark leather pants. He
waves his pink tail at the audience, and

with ocean-size smiles the four judges
float to their huge clamshell seats.

"Oh no. Not this."

I look around at the sound of Dad's
voice. He and Mom are swimming in from
the kitchen. I grip the remote control tightly.

"I was hoping to catch some of my interview on the news," Dad says. Dad is mayor of Shark Point, and there's nothing he likes better than seeing himself on jellyfishion.

Mom flops down on to the sea-sponge sofa and groans. "Harry, do we have to watch this trash?"

Most weeks I wouldn't have minded. I mean, there are only so many times you can watch a fish being told he sings like a ship's horn that's got a seagull stuck in it. But this week . . . oh, man . . . this week I *have* to see the special guest who's opening the show.

We've been talking about it all week at school. Me, Ralph (my pilot-fish friend) and Joe (my jellyfish pal) have been finding it really difficult to concentrate in class. In the end, our teachers had to ban anyone from even mentioning *The Shark Factor.*

"But, Mom," I say, "I *have* to watch it tonight."

"Why?" she says, looking puzzled.

I let out a massive sigh. "Seriously, Mom, if you were any more uncool, we'd have to stick you on an iceberg. Gregor the Gnasher is singing his *first ever* single tonight."

My stomach is doing little flips just thinking about it. Gregor the Gnasher is a great white shark and my number-one hero. Not only is he the Underwater Wrestling Champion of the World (signature move: the fin-chop with tail-driver), he's also an action-movie star and now he's breaking into the music business as a rapper called G-White.

Tonight's performance has been the talk of the interwet, and the number of 'GREGOR' fan pages on Plaicebook has tripled in two days—making the system crash.

Marcus Sea-cow floats up from behind his desk.

"Ladies and gentlefish, welcome to *The Shark Factor!*"

The crowd goes wild.

Marcus Sea-cow grins and gestures to the stage. "And now, opening the show with his debut single, 'Bite It,' please welcome the one, the only, Geeeeeeeeeee-White!"

Horns ring out across the stage. Then comes the beat of drums. Search-lights start flashing through the water. A huge, glittery curtain opens at the back of the stage and there's Gregor, floating fin-high on a column of bubbles. Two dolphins wearing shiny dresses are dancing on either side of him. Around his neck is a big gold shark's tooth, hanging on a gold chain that's so thick, it looks as

if it came from the anchor of a cruise ship. He's wearing a red Shike track-suit with diamond-encrusted sneakers on each fluke of his tail.

Oh, man!

The audience has gone crazy. I sneak my tail toward the remote to turn the volume up. Sea-cow, Barnacle, Electra, and Snapper float up above their judges' desk and start clapping along.

G-White nods to the beat as the dolphins sway beside him.

"I've got a big bite cuz I'm a great white," he raps.

I have to put my fin across my mouth to stop myself from squealing like a girl-shark.

"Great white!" the audience shouts back to him.

G-White grins, showing every single one of his three thousand and seventeen teeth. "I love causing FRIGHT, cuz I'm a great white!"

"Great white!" I join in with the audience.

"He's not too bright, he's a goofy great white," Dad mutters.

Huh?

I turn around and glare at Dad. He's shaking his head as he looks at the screen.

"Well, look at him," Dad says. "He might have lots of teeth, but I bet he couldn't think his way out of a wet paper bag."

"Dad!"

"Oh, come on, Harry. It's not exactly poetry, is it?" Dad says. "In my day we had real singers. Fish like Sting Ray and Sealion Dion. Now she could reach those high notes. This fool couldn't pitch a tent, let alone a tune."

Now Mom's shaking her head too. "I really don't know what anyone sees in that ridiculous big tooth-head. He's all teeth and no pants."

I can feel myself getting *really* angry

now. I've been looking forward to this all week, and now they're ruining it. "Be quiet!" I hiss. "I want to hear the chorus."

But they won't clam up.

"*Bite it*? Is that all he can sing about? Being mean? I don't think that's a very good example to be setting for the youngsters of Shark Point," Dad says in his "serious" voice.

"He's not mean!" I protest. "Not really."

"Gulp in ONE BITE, cuz I'm a great white!" screams G-White from the jelly-fishion.

Mom and Dad just look at me.

I'm torn. I just want to listen to the
song, but I feel like I have to defend
Gregor. He is my hero after all. I want
to be like him. Even if the only thing I
could gulp with one bite is a minnow.
Actually, I couldn't even manage that

when I met Marmaduke the Minnow, my new friend. That doesn't matter, I tell myself. I have to convince Mom and Dad that G-White is a good shark now.

I open my mouth to continue the argument, but Mom holds up her fin.

"Not another word, Harry," says Mom. "I think we should turn to another channel; I'm really not happy about you watching this. Great whites shouldn't even be allowed on jellyfishion, the way they frighten communities. It's a disgrace."

"But Gregor isn't like that anymore,

18

Mom. He hasn't eaten anyone for two years, seven months, and eleven days!"

"No, Harry. I'm sorry," Mom grabs the remote from my fin and flicks the jelly-fishion channel.

"Oh, Hubert."

"Oh, Gloria."

Oh no! It's *Drownton Abbey*! Two terribly fancy crabs are having a terribly fancy conversation, while doing some terribly fancy kissing, in the terribly fancy drawing room of a TERRIBLY TERRIBLE COSTUME DRAMA!

"Mom, it's just an act! Gregor isn't scary. He just pretends to be!"

"Well," Dad says, "he's scaring us by polluting the waves with his awful noise."

I can tell that they're not going to let me see the rest of the performance. The thing I've been waiting for the whole entire week is ruined.

"You two just don't understand!"

I swim up from the chair and swish out of the den, slamming the door behind me. I go straight to my room and throw myself onto the bed.

"It's not fair!" I shout, with a couple of prickly tears in my eyes trying hard to get out. I wipe them away with the tips of my fins. Then I beat my fins on the bed.

Barrap! Barrap! they go as they hit the seaweed blanket.

Hmmm.

Actually, that's not a bad beat.

Barrap, barrap.

Thud. Thud. Swish! goes my tail.

That rhythm's pretty good, I think to myself. Suddenly, I feel a little bit better. Maybe I've discovered a cool new talent. Maybe I'm not so different from G-White after all. I mean, he's a huge great white wrestling, movie, and singing star, and I'm just a little nobody hammerhead, but what if I can rap too?

Barrap! Barrap! go my fins.

Swish. Thud. Thud! goes my tail.

"I'm a hammerrrrrrrrrrrrrhead. And that's a bit bad actuallyyyyyy," I rap.

It didn't even rhyme.

I try again. A little faster on the bar-raps this time.

"H-h-h-h-hammerhead. I'm kinda blue if you look at me in the right light, and sometimes nearly red."

No, I'm not. I'm never red. That's just really silly.

I need something better that rhymes with hammerhead.

Lots of cool things rhyme with great white. That's why G-White's rap sounded so good. I have to think. . . .

"Hammerhead . . . hammerhead . . . sounds just like jam and sea-bread."

That is clearly the worst rap in the history of the world. Ever.

And then I hear someone laughing.

I look up from the bed, and see Larry, my lantern-fish night-light, and Humphrey, my humming-fish alarm clock. They're both rolling on the floor, clutching their sides and giggling like crazy at my dorky attempts to rap like G-White.

"Stop laughing!" I yell.

Larry looks at me, his lantern flashing on and off as he chuckles. "You mean you weren't trying to be funny?"

"No!"

"Are you sure?" asks Humphrey, buzzing away happily.

"Yes!"

Larry and Humphrey help each other off the floor, both trying—and failing—not to laugh.

"Be quiet, you two!" I shout, pulling the seaweed blanket over my hammer. "I'm trying to sleep."

But I can still hear them giggling

as they swim back to the shelf above my bed. Great. I bet G-White's alarm clock and lamp don't ever laugh at him.

Sometimes it really stinks being a hammerhead shark. Sometimes it's even worse. And then there are days like today, when just about everything goes wrong and it's worse than worse can be. As I drift off to sleep, I hope that some day I'll finally get to meet Gregor the Gnasher. If I met Gregor, he could show me how to wrestle, or act, or rap. . . .

Then no one would laugh at me.

I bet he could teach me stuff that would blow Larry and Humphrey and my mean parents out of the water!

But until then, I'm just going to be a dull hammerhead—that NOTHING COOL RHYMES WITH!

CHAPTER 2

In the morning I can't wait to get out of the house. Even though it's Sunday, and Sundays are usually boring in Shark Point. Mom and Dad don't even notice that I'm not talking to them over breakfast. They seem to have completely forgotten that they upset me last night.

Dad's writing a speech as his break-fast goes cold, and Mom keeps tickling me behind my hammer and calling me her "little starfish." I just stare into my bowl of kelp krispies and bite my lip. I bite it a bit too hard as Mom tickles me again.

"Ouch!" I say.

No one notices.

Great.

I bet this doesn't happen in G-White's house. I bet everyone notices the second he gets mad about something. I leave my bowl on the table to show them how angry I am. But Mom just picks it up and puts it in the dishwasher without saying a thing.

It's like I don't exist!

I grab my jacket and head over to Ralph's. At least he'll be glad to see me.

Ralph lives in a block of coral apartments about five minutes swimming away from our house. But I get there even quicker than usual because:

1. It's Sunday so there's hardly any traffic on the roads.

2. I'm swimming extra fast because . . .

3. I'm still angry about what happened last night and . . .

4. I'm even angrier that at breakfast, Mom and Dad acted as if nothing happened.

Sometimes making a list helps me think more clearly and get my thoughts in order. This list doesn't. When I go over it again in my head, I feel even angrier and swim even faster.

I swish to a halt outside Ralph's bedroom window.

"Ralph!" I call. I wait a bit and the window opens. Ralph's head pokes out and he yawns.

"Morning," he says, rubbing his eyes and sliding slowly out of the window, still in his pajamas. It isn't like Ralph to be so sleepy. He's usually raring to go in the mornings because he wants to get his breakfast out of my mouth. Pilot fish eat the leftovers from between sharks' teeth, and yes, it is as gross as it sounds. To be honest, I'd rather have a toothbrush, but then how would Ralph eat? So I open my mouth and wait.

Ralph yawns again, and quickly pokes around, pulling out a few half-eaten kelp krispies. He chews them slowly.

"What's up with you?" I ask.

"Late night," he says between little yawns. "I must have watched G-White about a hundred times on rewind. It was awesome, wasn't it?"

I start feeling angry about last night, so I try to change the subject as quickly as I can. "Yeah, awesome. So what should we do today?"

Ralph gives yet another yawn. "Sorry,

Harry. I've got homework to finish before tomorrow. I was supposed to do it last night, but I was too busy watching G-White. Mom says I have to do it today."

Great.

"Why don't you go and see what Joe's doing?" says Ralph, scratching his belly and swimming slowly back up to his bedroom window. "See you at lunchtime, okay?" He disappears inside without even waiting for a reply.

I'm furious.

We always get together on Sunday mornings. But now Ralph can't make it *because he stayed up too late watching G-White.*

I swim away in a huff, darting through town as fast as I can. By the time I get to Joe's family's cave I'm a little bit calmer, but not much.

I ring the bell and through the hanging fronds I see Joe float up to the entrance. He bumps into the wall and looks at me with bleary eyes.

"Yo!" he says slowly, with a yawn.

I can see exactly where this is going. "Up late watching *The Shark Factor*, right?" I ask.

Joe nods and his body changes

from yellow to light green, the color he always goes when he's really, really tired.

"Yeah, it was awesome, wasn't it? We watched it over and over again. Well, I was behind the sofa at the beginning because those explosions were a bit loud, but otherwise it was GREAT!" Joe sticks out his tentacles and scowls, in an

impression of G-White when he was floating on the column of bubbles. "I'm thinking of changing my name to Jel-Fish. What do you think?"

If I say anything, it will just be nasty, so instead I nod and try to put on a convincing smile.

Joe relaxes a few of his tentacles. "Yeah, I think it suits me too."

If I grit my teeth any harder, I think I might break them. "Are you coming out?" I manage to say.

Joe shakes his head. "Sorry, bro, Jel-Fish gotta stay in his crib and help the parental unit with the house."

"You mean your mom wants you to clean your bedroom?" I say.

"Truth."

I can't stay a second longer or I'll explode, so I wave good-bye and swim away in a double . . . no . . . *triple* huff.

It seems I'm the only person in Shark Point not to have seen the jellyfishion event of the year. All because my parents are the uncoolest parents in the ocean. As if it isn't bad enough having a head shaped like a hammer, now everyone will think I'm 100 percent more dorky because I didn't get to see G-White.

I swim down to the park, but it's

empty. Everyone's still in bed then. Great. I swim on.

It seems like the whole town is taking a long time to wake up and get going, even for a Sunday. The stores are deserted and I'm getting more and more bored. I'm getting so bored that I'd even be happy to see Rick Reef and Donny Dogfish, my two least favorite sharks. Even Donny snickering while Rick FLUBBERS my head would be better than this.

My tail is starting to ache and I realize I've been swimming around too fast for too long. I decide to rest for a bit. I'm by my

school now and I can see that the play-grounds are empty, so I swim down to the finball goalposts and lean back against the net.

I wonder what G-White is doing after his performance last night. Is he wandering around his hometown like Billy No-Friends feeling all down in the dumps? Of course he isn't. He's probably in his gold-plated hot spring, scrubbing his back with gold-plated scrubbing brushes while gold-plated pilot fish delicately pick the leftover caviar from between his gold-plated teeth.

Humph. I turn around and bury my hammer in the net.

"It's worse than being dead, being a ham-ham-hammer head," I whisper to myself. "I should've stayed in bed. I'm a ham-ham-hammerhead."

I flex my fins. I want to pound the ground with them.

"What kind of lyrics are they?" some-one calls out from behind me.

Huh?

"They're, like, totally the worst lyrics EVAH!"

I flip around and see Cora and Pearl, the dolphin twins. They must have swum up behind me while I was trying out my latest useless rap.

Cora and Pearl strike poses. They look just like G-White's backup singers.

"If you wanna do lyrics right . . . , " says Pearl.

"You gotta sing about love," says Cora, and they high-fin each other.

"You gotta get smoochy-woochy." Pearl blows a kiss at Cora, who takes a picture of her on her SeaPhone.

"You gotta get lovey with the dovey." Cora puckers her lips and flutters her eyelashes as Pearl takes a picture of her. Pretty soon their camera-phones are flashing almost as much as the lights on *The Shark Factor* last night.

I think I'm going to be sick. I start to

swim away, but the camera flashes are following me.

"Don't you want us to help you, Harry?" says Cora as she swims alongside me.

I say nothing. I don't want to be mean. It's not their fault I didn't get to see G-White last night. I just want to be left on my own to sulk.

Pearl starts to rap while Cora drums her fins on her stomach. "Harry wants to sing, but he ain't got a thing. Bring it."

I swim out of the school grounds toward the Point, but the twins don't look like they're going to leave me alone.

They're having far too much fun rapping about me.

"Harry, don't run away—listen to what we say. Word."

Hopefully they'll leave me alone soon. I swim on like crazy, trying to get away from them. But Cora and Pearl swim after me, laughing and singing. I stick my fins in my ears, but I can still hear them.

I'm at the Point now. There's nowhere else to go except the deep ocean. If I just

45

ignore the twins, maybe they'll go away.

Or maybe they won't. Maybe today is going to be even worse than yesterday!

And then something catches my eye. Out in the dark wall of water beyond the Point I see a huge shadow.

I take my fins out of my ears.

"Don't look so sad; you're really not that bad."

"Yes, he is."

"I know—I just wanted a rhyme."

"Shhh!" I say. "Look!"

I point toward the shadow. It's big and getting bigger. I squint into the darkness.

Oh, man!

It's a great white.

And it's coming this way.

But it's not just *any* great white.

I'd know that shape anywhere.

It's GREGOR!

CHAPTER 3

"It's a great white!" I yell.

But before I can say that I think it's Gregor, the twins start SCREAMING.

"We're under attack! We're under attack!"

CRASH!

That's Cara knocking into my left

hammer as they rush to get away.

"Wait!" I yell. My head is stinging and my stomach feels like a washing machine as I spin around and around. "He's not going to hurt you."

But it's too late. I manage to stop myself spinning and see the twins racing back toward town screaming, "We're all going to die! We're all going to die!"

I look back over my shoulder. Gregor is still moving toward me through the water. But I can't stay and talk to my hero.

I've got to find Pearl and Cora. I've got to stop them.

I try to use my hammer-vision to locate a fast-moving current to ride on. Dolphins and hammerheads are both fast swimmers, but Pearl and Cora have had a good head start and I'm still dizzy from all the spinning.

Unfortunately, it seems that the lazy Sunday feeling of the town has spread to the water, as the currents are all really slow. I'll just have to kick my tail as hard as I can.

My muscles are starting to cramp from all the swimming I've already done this morning. But I can't stop. I need to catch up with the twins. I kick even faster and feel myself surge through the ocean. I'm going almost as fast as Gregor! I can do this! I'm sure I can get to them before they cause any panic.

Or maybe not.

As I reach the main road, I see fish, sharks, and crabs coming out of their houses and stores. Some are still in their pajamas. Some little kids are crying, and their moms and dads are putting their fins around them.

"Have you seen them?" a squid calls to me as I zoom past.

"Seen what?"

"The school of great whites. The twins said they're about to attack Shark Point!"

Oh no! This is worse than I thought.

Panic is spreading through the town. A turtle bus coming in from the Crabton road has clearly tried to turn around and crashed into the side of a supermarket. It looks like all the passengers and the turtle are okay, but the coral wall of the supermarket has a huge hole in it, and loads of bags of piranha puffs are drifting out into the water.

I swim on.

In the distance I catch a glimpse of

Cora and Pearl as they reach Seahorse Square. If they've caused this amount of panic just going up the main road, who knows what's going to happen next!

I kick on, ignoring the pain in my tail and fins and the burning in my gills.

Cora and Pearl disappear around the corner. All I can hear is the buzz of conversation from the fish and sharks in the street. The number-one topic is "Shark alert!"

When I get to Seahorse Square, there's already a crowd gathering around Cora and Pearl. Fish, dolphins, crabs, and sharks. The dolphin twins are outside

the mayor's office, banging on the door.

"What's all this noise about?" a voice shouts from the other side of the square.

Oh no!

It's Dad. He's got his mayor's chain around his neck. He pushes through the crowds toward his office. Mom is swimming behind him and her face looks all concerned. I can see that she's looking for me and she's really worried. I hold up my fin and wave to her, knowing exactly what's coming next.

Mom catches sight of me and her face lights up. "Angelfish! You're all right!"

"Yes, Mom, I'm fi—pshhhtttttthh!"

I'm trying to say that I'm fine, but she

swims across so fast and throws her fins around me so hard that my mouth is buried in her coat.

More and more fish are cramming into the square. Everyone seems terrified. I need to do something.

"I need to do something!" Dad says.

Huh?

He swims up above the crowd, waving his fins around.

"Citizens of Shark Point!"

Everyone ignores him and continues to panic.

"CITIZENS OF SHARK POINT!" Dad yells at the top of his gills.

Everyone still ignores him.

Mom lets me go. "WILL YOU ALL BE QUIET?!" she shouts. Silence falls.

Mom's using "the voice." It's the voice she uses to tell me off when I've been very bad. It's loud and it's scary. I hear a bottom tooting.

I look around, and see Joe blushing as he swims into the square. "Sorry!" he whispers.

He's followed by Ralph, Rick, and Donny.

It seems like the whole town is here. Rick takes a flubbery swipe at my hammer, but I manage to duck out of his way

and float nearer to Mom. He wouldn't dare to now, not when she's using "the voice."

"Citizens of Shark Point," Dad says again, a little calmer now. "We must not panic. We must be calm. We must not worry ourselves unnecessarily!"

"It's all right for you; you're a shark," a turtle calls from the crowd. "It's not you who's going to get eaten, is it?"

The shouting and the panicking start again. An old, ruddy-faced dolphin called Mr. Bottlenose brings Cora and Pearl forward. "Now, tell everyone what you saw, girls."

Cora trembles.

Pearl shakes.

"Well, w-w-w-we didn't really see anything," Cora stutters.

"H-H-H-H-Harry did," Pearl says, pointing at me.

It seems every eye in the square is now looking at me. I can feel my cheeks turning red.

"Oh, look, he's turning pink, just like a girl," Rick snickers to Donny.

Mr. Bottlenose swims up and looks at me. "Did you see great whites, boy?"

"Yes, but only—"

Before I have time to tell them the

rest, Mr. Bottlenose is spinning around, yelling, "It's true! It's true!"

"Um, if we could just calm down a bit," says Dad.

Mr. Bottlenose grabs my fin. "Take us

to them, boy," he bellows. "We've got to see what we're up against!"

With that, twelve strong dolphins come out of the crowd and follow as Mr. Bottlenose leads me back toward the edge of the Point. Mom and Dad swim after us.

"You've got to listen!" I plead, but Mr. Bottlenose waves me aside and swims on determinedly.

Ralph and Joe swim up beside me. "You had any lunch yet?" asks Ralph.

"Is that all you can think about?" I say.

"I'm starving! I hardly had any of

your kelp krispies earlier because I was so tired."

"Don't remind me," I say a bit grumpily. But I don't mind I missed *The Shark Factor* so much anymore, now that I know we're about to see Gregor in the flesh. And hopefully then everyone will calm down. Gregor is a superstar now—he's not going to eat *anyone*.

Eventually we get to the edge of the Point. Mr. Bottlenose pushes me forward. "Where are they, boy? Show us."

I flick on my hammer-vision and scan the dark water ahead. "Mr. Bottlenose, please, it's not—"

"No need to be scared, boy," Mr. Bottlenose interrupts. "Just show us where you saw them and we'll do the rest."

The strong dolphins are rolling up their shirtsleeves and getting ready for trouble.

PING!

My hammer-vision bursts into life and starts giving me information.

Gregor's still here! And he's coming toward us.

PING! Fifty feet and closing.

PING!!! Forty feet and closing.

"What can you sense, boy? Tell us!" Mr. Bottlenose yells.

"It's a great white, all right," I say. "And it's coming this way . . . but, Mr. Bottlenose, you must listen to me, it's only Gre—pshhhttttttthh."

That's Mom, pulling me into her coat again. "Don't worry, my little starfish. I'll protect you!"

"But li—pshhhttttttthh! It's okay, we're not in any da—pshhhttttttthh!"

I give up.

The strong dolphins have all formed a line on the edge of the Point, protecting the crowds of fish and sharks behind them. My hammer-vision is *PINGING* like crazy.

64

We can all see the shadow coming toward us out of the gloom. It's the biggest shark I've ever seen.

It must be Gregor. But then . . .

"Sea-flowers for sale, sea-flowers!

Who will buy my lover-ly sea-flowers?"

Huh?

Double "huh?"

TRIPLE "HUH?"!

Out of the gloom comes the shark. But it's *not* a great white.

It's a great big basking shark! She's wearing a long floral dress and a floppy fern hat, and carrying a huge bag of flowers. "Oh, who will buy my lover-ly sea-flowers? Bouquet of sea urchins? Vase of coral clusters?" she says.

The citizens of Shark Point aren't panicking anymore—they're laughing.

At me!

The basking shark can't stop grinning as the relieved townsfish rush up to her to buy her flowers.

FLUBBER!!!!

Rick boings my rubbery hammerhead

from behind. "Awesome hammer-vision, T-Bone face," he whispers in my jangling ear. "What's going to be next? Giant squids under all our beds?"

A new, horrible list starts writing itself in my mind.

1. I can't rap.
2. I'VE GOT A STUPID HEAD!
3. My hammer-vision isn't working properly anymore.

My hammer-vision was the ONLY cool thing about being a hammerhead. Now everyone thinks it doesn't work.

There are now exactly ZERO cool things about being a hammerhead shark.

ZERO cool things about being ME!

CHAPTER 4

Cora and Pearl aren't talking to me. They blame *me* for the panic *they* caused in town yesterday.

Rick and Donny snicker and whisper every time they swim past me in the school hall.

Joe and Ralph are trying to be nice,

but I can tell they're a little bit embarrassed to be friends with the 'kid who cried great white,' as everyone on the jellyfishion news last night was calling me. You would think that Mom and Dad would be trying to cheer me up, but no. They've been too busy trying to get Dad on jellyfishion so that he can tell everyone what a great mayor he was yesterday.

When I get to my desk in class, I see that someone has drawn a big bunch of flowers on it.

Great.

I'm never gonna live this down.

Luckily, the first lesson after assembly is PE with Mr. Skim, our flying-fish teacher, and there's going to be a cross-seabed swim. At least that gives me a chance to make the other kids remember that I'm a fast shark with a great sense of direction (when my hammer-vision is working properly, that is).

Mr. Skim is waiting for us on the field, doing fin-ups in his shiny tracksuit. "Okay," he says, getting up as we file out of the locker rooms. "The route for today's cross-seabed swim is quite simple. From school you take the

coast road to the Point, go around the head-land, back across the coral marsh, then under Crabton Bridge, and back to school. Any questions?"

My stomach sinks as Rick raises a fin. "Mr. Skim, what should we do if we see any vicious, dolphin-eating, urchin-chewing, crab-killing, fish-feasting FLOWER SHARKS on the swim?"

Everyone, including Ralph, thinks this

is hilarious. If the seabed could open up and swallow me right now, I'd be the happiest hammerhead alive.

Mr. Skim smiles but doesn't play along. "Any *serious* questions?"

Rick and Donny are high-finning each other, and Cora and Pearl are typing something on their SeaPhones. Probably putting Rick's joke up on Plaicebook.

Great.

Mr. Skim blows his whistle, and the swim is underway.

I kick away with my tail as fast as I can. Normally I would swim slower to be with Ralph and Joe—they're not as fast as me

and I don't like to leave them behind. But today, I just want to get my hammer down and swim as fast as I can. My face feels waaaaaaay red after Rick's joke, and the faster I go, the cooler the sea water is, taking the heat out of my cheeks.

I get to the Point in record time, just ahead of the leading pack. Rick's a very fast swimmer, but I think he's too busy fooling around with Donny and showing off to the dolphin twins to keep up with me today. I sneak a look behind me, and see him swimming on his back, blowing bubbles out of his gills at Cora and Pearl who are laughing their heads off.

I kick on.

Over the Point and on to . . .

Oh, blubber!

I can't remember which way Mr. Skim wanted us to go. Was it around the headland first, or down across the coral marsh? If Rick and the others see me going back to ask directions, I'll never hear the end of it. "Harry's had another hammer-vision epic fail!" I can almost see their Plaicebook status updates now.

I zoom down onto the coral marsh, convinced that I'm going in the right direction. I kick on and on, determined to get to the finish line first.

The water is getting warmer. I can feel it on my face.

Double blubber!

I should have taken more time to think about the route. It would have been the headland first, before the coral marsh, because from the Point, the coral marsh route will take me straight toward . . .

The shallows.

This is the one place that none of us are allowed to go, except accompanied by an adult. As the spongy coral marsh thins out, the seabed becomes sandy and shallow. The light becomes much brighter, and the water much warmer.

The chances of bumping into human beings, or leggy air-breathers as we call them, are really increased here.

But if I turn around, and go back the way I came, I'm going to be last in the cross-seabed swim.

I *can't* be last.

What should I do?

Then I have an idea. If I continue on, right across the shallows, there's a coral channel that doubles back and comes right out at the Crabton Bridge. If I go as fast as I can, I could use that instead of going around the headland, and still win the race.

Smart!

I swish my tail and start swimming at double speed.

The seabed is leveling out. The water is heating up like a lovely relaxing hot spring, and the sunlight glitters all around. It's a shame we don't get to go to the shallows very often, it's a really beautiful and welcoming place. . . .

PING!

Huh?

My emergency hammer-vision is kicking in at the first sign of danger. Up above me is a huge shadow blocking out the sun. Suddenly, I'm in a shaft of cold water, and I don't know if I'm shivering from the cold or from fear.

Probably both!

The shadow is big and black as it skims through the water. My hammer-vision is *PINGING* off the scale. I slam to a halt. There's only one thing that shadow can be.

A shark.

I listen to hear if it's selling flowers.

Nothing. No sound at all.

A huge shark cutting silently through the water can only be up to one thing.

Hunting.

And a shadow that big can only be from one kind of hunter.

A GREAT WHITE!

Now I'm torn.

Do I want to go on and win the race, or should I go back, get the others, and show them that I *do* know a great white when I see one?

Oh, man . . .

Okay. I can win a race ANYTIME, but this might be my only chance to show them that my hammer-vision *does* work!

I turn around, hurrying out of the shallows and back across the coral marsh.

I'm imagining the twins' Plaicebook updates once I prove to them that my hammer-vision works. . . .

I zoom out of the marsh and slam hard into Ralph and Joe, who are still slow-coaching their way down from the Point to the headland.

"Hey!" says Ralph.

Pop. Pop. Pop. Pop, says Joe's rear. "Watch it!" he manages to yell before his arms and fronds curl up into sea-horse tails in my wake.

"Shark!" I say breathlessly, pointing back over the coral marsh. "Shark!"

"Yeah, right, what's this one selling?

Dolls?" Rick has appeared with Donny behind Ralph and Joe.

"I don't have time to argue—there's a great white shark! A big one—in the shallows!"

Ralph looks puzzled. "What were you doing in the shallows? That's not on the route."

"I took a wrong turn."

Rick and Donny are giggling bubbles into the water. "Hammer-vision gone wrong again?" says Rick.

"If you don't believe me, why don't you come and have a look for yourself?" I press my nose right into Rick's face.

He looks a bit shocked. "All right. Show us."

I lead the way, pulling Ralph by the fin, and feeling Joe cling to my tail with several of his many tentacles.

Rick and Donny follow, but at a safe distance. They're not as brave as they pretend to be.

We burst out of the coral marsh and head up toward the shallows. The weather up above the sea seems to be getting worse. There are lots of clouds now, and the water is full of shadows. It's going to be hard to spot the . . .

But yes—right above us—the *huge* shadow!

"There it is!"

Ralph, Joe, Rick, and Donny look to where I'm pointing.

And that's when the sun comes out from behind the bank of clouds.

86

And then I see Donny, Rick, and Ralph start to laugh.

Joe just giggles out of his rear.

Huh?

I look back up.

Oh.

No.

In the bright sunlight, the shark is revealed in all its glory.

Its pink glory.

Its plastic glory.

Its girly pink plastic shark-shaped glory.

It's a raft. One of those plastic blow-up things used by the leggy air-breathers to float on the water.

It's not a shark.

And now I'm so uncool, you could fry sea-cucumber fritters on my face.

Ralph stops laughing when he sees my shoulders slump. Then he pokes Joe, who immediately stops tooting.

Rick swims so close to me, I can count the go-faster stripes on his track-suit. "Nice one, Harry. You can't even tell a great white shark from a raft. Wait until everyone at school hears about this!"

89

Rick and Donny high-fin, and swim away laughing.

I can't believe I've been so dopey. Again!

CHAPTER 5

When school finally finishes, I sneak past the field, darting behind clumps of sea plants. I just want to get away as quickly as possible without being seen. Rick, Donny, Ralph, and Joe are playing finball with some other kids from class. Normally I'd stop and play too.

Not tonight.

Not after the day I've had.

Everywhere I went today, in every class, fish have been pulling my fin about the raft—even Mrs. Shelby. When Mr. Gape, our basking-shark librarian, came in, she said, "Now don't worry, Harry, there's no need to be scared. I know he looks like another type of shark. . . . "

You know you're in trouble when *teachers* are laughing at you.

I slink away from school and the happy sounds of the finballers. Rick has just scored a curling net-ripper and everyone is going crazy cheering. The dolphin twins are singing "Ra ra ra, Rick!" like cheerleaders on the sideline.

Well, that's okay.

I don't need friends. I don't need anyone to play finball with.

I bet G-White doesn't care about friends. Why would he, now he's a famous wrestler, movie star, and rapper?

And one day, I'm gonna be just like that.

H-Hed. That's what I'll call myself. That's a great name for a . . .

Sigh.

Yeah.

It's *totally* awful. I can't even come up with a good rapper's name. I might as well just give up.

When I get home, Mom's bustling around the kitchen making snacks. I hang up my book bag and coat, thinking that at least today can't get any worse.

"Oh, good!" Mom calls out when she sees me. "I need you to go to the newsstand." She goes over to her finbag and takes out some money. "I didn't get a chance to pick up my *True Love Forever* magazine earlier, and it always sells out really quickly. Can you go out and buy me one while I finish my snack?"

Why is it that whenever I think a day can't get any worse, it always does?

Now, hammer-vision-fail-raft-spotter-boy is going to have to swim to the newsstand and ask for a copy of *True Love Forever* magazine. Knowing  my luck, Cora and Pearl will be there, filming it on their SeaPhones to upload straight onto CrewTube.

But if this doesn't go wrong, then something tomorrow is bound to.

So what's the point in fighting it?

I put out my fin for the money.

"Make sure it's this week's though," Mom says. "The one with the bright pink cover and the free Twilight Trout Pout lipstick."

Great.

I swim out of the house and off to the main road, my heart nose-diving with doom.

I can tell everyone's looking at me as I swim slowly along. I've been all over the news for two days now—I'm the laughing stock of Shark Point.

A prawn whizzing by on a

skateboard asks me if I'm on my way to the optician's to get my hammer-vision tested.

I ignore him.

A hermit crab puts his pincers over his head in an arch. "Look out, I'm a great white!" He laughs so hard, his shell falls off.

I ignore him, too. If this goes on much longer, I'll be ignoring all of Shark Point.

Thankfully, there's no one else around when I get to the newsstand, since it's on a quiet side street. The store after the newsstand is the Wet Pet Shop. Usually when I come here, I press my hammer up at the window to look at the kittenfish in their tanks. But today I can't be bothered. I just want to buy the magazine and get the embarrassment over and done with.

The Wet Pet Shop door is locked and there's a big "Gone Fishin" sign hanging on it. No wonder the street is so quiet—if the Wet Pet Shop is closed, there's hardly any reason for anyone to come down here.

Finally, my luck seems to be chang-ing. I'm just about to take the magazine from the newsstand when . . .

Grrrrrrrrrrrrr!

Wow, my stomach is rumbling like crazy. I hadn't even realized I was hungry.

Grrrrrrrrrrrrrrrrrrrrrrr!

I don't think it's ever rumbled so loud in my life.

Grrrrrrrrrrrrrrrrrrrrrrrrrrrrrrrr!!!

But hang on a minute, I don't think the low growling, grumbling, rumbling noise is coming from my stomach after all.

PING!

My hammer-vision starts going off.

PING!

PING!!!

"Yeah, right. So what is it this time? A rubber pacifier with teeth?" I say.

PING!

PING!!

PING!!!

I have a look around on the main road, but I can't see anything wrong. It must be COMPLETELY broken. Great. I'm a hammerhead with no hammer-vision.

Annoyed, I glance back the way I came and nearly do a double fin-flip in shock. This time, there *IS* a great white!

It's huge, it looks super mean, and it's hanging above the Wet Pet Shop, staring down at the window. But it's not about to go "Awwwwwwww" at the kittenfish. It's licking its lips and it's

Grrrrrrrrrrrrrring, getting ready to go in for the kill!

I have to do something! I have to say something!

"H-h-h-h-hello. H-h-h-h-h-h-how are you?"

Yes, I know it's nonsense and I sound like I'm terrified. But that's because I am terrified, and I don't know what else to say.

In the window, the kittenfish are trying to hide under each other.

"Shut it, kid, can't you see I'm busy?" the great white growls. "I'm about to have my snack. Shouldn't you be going home to get yours?"

102

The great white starts dropping slowly in the water, licking his lips and winding up his tail.

"You don't get your snack from the Wet Pet Shop." My heart starts beating a million times too fast in my chest.

The great white looks at me with his big black eyes.

"Where else am I going to get live kittenfish? I love the way they wriggle as they go down my throat."

The kittenfish start getting more panicky in their tank, swimming around in circles, squeaking and mewing. This just seems to make the great white even more excited. He opens his mouth and gnashes his teeth.

I look around for anyone else who can come and help. But the street is still deserted.

I dart back up to the main road, desperate to tell someone, *anyone*, what's going on. I swim up to a whale and her kids.

"Quick! Down there! There's a great white!" I gasp.

The whale just smiles and pats me on the head. "Yes, of course there is, dear. I don't think you're going to get us with that one again. Nice try though!"

"But—"

The whale just swims on, with her kids finning their noses at me.

Oh no!

I dodge some turtle-cars and go up to an octopus who is looking in a jeweller's window at eight-holed engagement rings.

"Help!" I shout, shaking him by the tentacle. "There's a great white at the Wet Pet Shop! He's about to eat the kittenfish!"

The octopus turns and looks at me. "Forget it, kid. I heard all about your great white prank on the jellyfishion." He blows ink in my face and goes back to looking in the window.

I dart up and down the street, looking

for someone else to tell. I'm near the side street when I hear . . .

CRASH!

It's coming from the Wet Pet Shop.

The great white must be starting his attack!

CRASH!

I start swimming faster. I can't leave the kittenfish to him. I have to do something to stop them from becoming the great white's snack—even if it means I end up becoming his dessert!

CHAPTER 6

I know that this really isn't the best time to make a list. But a list of things that make me happy will make me feel less scared. As the great white winds himself up to smash into the Wet Pet Shop door again, I start listing like crazy in my head.

1. **Kelp krispies**. I like them! I'm so close to the great white now. I can see a piece of seaweed trapped between his teeth.

2. **Ralph**. He's great. I like him! I'm so close to the great white now. I can see a tattoo on his dorsal fin saying: **FIGHT 4 THE RIGHT TO BITE**.

3. **Joe**. He's great too! I'm so close to the great white now. I'm actually in between him and the shop!

4. **And Mom and Dad**. I love them, too! I really, really love them!

I've reached the end of my list.

"STOP!" I shout as loudly and as scar-ily as I can.

The great white is all coiled up, ready to smash into the door of the Wet Pet Shop for a final time, as the hinges are just about to give way. He pauses for a moment. He stares at me with his huge, black, mean-looking eyes.

"You again? What did I tell you a minute ago, kid? Get out of the way or you're in big trouble."

"Kittenfish? What kind of cowardly shark eats kittenfish? Well, obviously a coward with all the bravery of a dead haddock." I cannot believe what just came out of my mouth. Now I'm dessert for sure.

"What did you say?" growls the great white.

Oh well, if I'm going to be a great white's dessert I suppose I've got nothing left to lose. "Are you deaf as well as a coward? Or just *out to lunch*?"

Oh. MY. COD!

"GRRRRRRRRRRRRRRRRRRRRRRRR-
RRRRRRRRRRRRRRRRRRRRRR!!!!!"

The great white lets his wound-up tail go and leaps straight at me.

But that's exactly what I wanted. "Catch me if you can!" I yell, and I'm off too.

Zooooooooooooooooooooooooom!
PING!!! PING!!!

I know, hammer-vision! I know!

I shoot off toward the main road, knowing the great white will follow.

My hammer-vision clicks automatically to ESCAPE MODE. I hope this time it doesn't let me down.

ZOOOOM! I shoot round the corner. A

112

turtle taxi screeches to a halt as I shoot on to the road.

"Watch where you're going!" screams the taxi driver, waving his flipper with anger.

"GREAT WHITE!" I scream as I dart over him.

"Just you wait 'til I tell your dad the mayor about this!" the driver shouts. "You're going to be grounded for . . . for . . . for . . ."

The great white zooms out of the side street after me, and the turtle's jaw drops down in shock. "For . . . for . . . for . . . It's a GREAT WHITE!"

"That's what I *said*!" I cry as I shoot down the street with the great white snapping at my tail. As I go, faces change from smiles and laughter to total terror as they see what's snarling away behind me.

Fish dive into store doorways, squids slide under turtles. Outside

Guppy's Grocery Store boxes of sea fruit get smashed into the air by my hammer-head, and telephone poles get knocked over by the wild flapping of the great white's huge tail.

I can tell from the currents in the water that he's gaining on me.

"I'm gonna chew you up and spit you out, boy!" the great white shouts.

"You've got to catch me first!" I yell behind me.

My hammer-vision escape mode is pinging away, warning me of any obstacles. A turtle bus from Crabton pulls out in front of me and I squeeze under it. The great white has to go over.

I swim off the street out toward the Point. A school of minnows is returning from a class outing. I skirt around the side of the group. The great white is too big to swerve that quickly and he ploughs on straight ahead. Luckily, the teacher, an old hermit crab with little glasses and a knitted sweater, has pushed all the young fish aside, and the great white just sails through.

I'm kicking and kicking, turning this way and that. But the great white is still gaining on me. I'm trying to think of ways to shake him off.

I turn a sick full 180 half-fin, and barrel

into a reverse tail-endy. This sends the great white flying over my head, and suddenly I'm heading away from the Point in the opposite direction.

I'm starting to get tired now, so I know I won't be able to keep this up for long.

"Come here!" the great white bellows, finally managing to change direction and follow me again.

I don't know what I'm going to do. I've managed to lead the great white away from town, but now what?

PING!

My hammer-vision is looking

waaaaaaaaaaaaaaay ahead. It zooms the school playground right into view.

I can see Rick and the others still playing finball, and my hammer-vision super senses send me faint sounds of Cora and Pearl, still cheerleading.

I can't go right, because that will take me over the coral marsh.

I can't go left, because that will take me out into the wide ocean.

I can't go back, because the great white will just eat me!

I've got to go on, but that means I'm going to lead the great white . . . *straight to my friends!*

"Great white!" I scream as the play-ground gets closer and closer.

I can see Rick about to take one of his fancy-pants free kicks with the fin-ball. Everyone else is concentrating on that, rather than me and the great white shooting toward them at top speed!

"GREAT WHITE!" I yell again at the top of my voice.

"Pipe down, Harry! Can't you see I'm concentrating?" Rick calls over his shoulder. He continues lining up the ball.

We're almost there. I can feel the vibrations in the water as the great white's jaws chomp after my tail. I can

feel the hot, hungry breath blowing from his gills.

What am I going to do?

Rick takes a float back. He's ready to kick.

Ralph is floating between the goal posts, wearing goalkeeping gloves on his fins. He's focusing hard on Rick, getting ready to try and save the ball.

"OUCH!"

The great white is nipping at my flukes.

"I can almost taste you, kid!" he snarls.

Ralph looks over Rick's head—straight at me and the great white.

"Great white!" he yells.

"You won't fool me with lame-o tricks like your goofy friend," Rick sneers.

"Great white!" calls Joe. *"Pop pop pop pop pop pop,"* calls his rear.

"Oh, zip it!" Rick yells.

"Ra ra ra," the dolphin twins sing. "Ra ra raaaaggghhhhh!" the dolphin twins scream as they turn to look at what Ralph and Joe are looking at. Me—being chased by a great big great white.

Rick starts swishing his tail angrily. "It's my free kick. Stop trying to ruin it!"

"Rick!" yells Donny, pointing wildly with his fin. "LOOK!"

And finally Rick *does* look.

And then he just about breaks the sea-speed record for hiding behind twin dolphins with your rear tooting like a motorboat!

"GREAT WHITE!" he screams as he flies behind Pearl and Cora.

"I know!" I scream back as I skim low across the field. And then an idea pings into my head even louder than my hammer-vision. I start waving my fins madly at Ralph in the goal.

"Ralph! Get out the way!" I yell.

Ralph dives to the left, covering his head with his fins.

I've got just one chance for my plan to work. I head straight for the goal, kicking as hard and as fast as I can. The great white's hot gill-breath is sending shivers up my spine.

The goal posts come up really fast. I hold out my fins and curl my whole body into a sharky body-knot. I grab the top of the post with my fin and hope that my speed will be enough to carry me around. It is. I spin around the post, up over the crossbar, and as I come around I flick out both flukes of my tail as hard as I can.

CRACK!!!

The great white's nose connects perfectly with my tail-flick. The nose is where great whites keep all their most sensitive hunting sensors and delicate S.H.A.R.K.D.A.R. equipment. It's also the most vulnerable place on a great white's body. If you're ever facing a great white, hit him as hard as you can on the nose.

BOIIIIIIIIIIIIINNNNNNNNNNNGG!

The great white's eyes snap shut and his body goes limp. He's traveling so fast that his whole body flies forward, knocking me aside as he shoots right into the goal.

ONE-ZERO HARRY!

The great white is completely uncon-
scious as he floats in the water, but he
won't be for long. I swim up, unhook the

net from the crossbar, and drape the net over him. Then, grabbing the net in my teeth, I swim around and around until he is totally tied up.

Done!

"Yaaaaaaaaaaaaaaaay!" cry the dolphin twins.

"Yessssssssssssssssssssssssssss!" cry Ralph and Joe.

"Has it gone yet?" whimpers Rick, still hiding behind Pearl and Cora.

And then it seems like the whole town is crowding on to the finball field, coming to see what's happened. At the head of the crowd are Mom and Dad.

Mom throws herself at me and gives me a massive hug. "Starfish! You've saved us all!"

For the first time ever, I'm not embarrassed by Mom calling me starfish. But that's probably because everyone is pointing at the great white trapped in the net and cheering like crazy.

Cheering ME!

Dad high-fins me, then raises my fin like I'm a champion wrestler. "I'm so proud of you, son," he says with a smile.

Ralph, Joe, Cora, Pearl, and even Donny the Dogfish are pushing their way through the crowd toward me. Ralph and

Joe can't stop smiling. Cora and Pearl are snapping away with the cameras on their SeaPhones. Donny is clapping and cheering! In the background I can see

Rick getting off the seabed and dusting himself off with his fins. He doesn't look happy at the attention I'm getting.

But I don't care. It's AWESOME.

"Harry's hammer-vision saved us all!" Dad shouts, and from the clapping and cheering it seems like the whole town agrees.

I can't believe it. Just this morning I was so down in the dumps that I wanted the seabed to swallow me whole. Now I'm on top of the ocean!

As everyone gathers around me, high-finning me and slapping me on the back, I realize something so shocking, it makes my goggly eyes spin. Ever since I can remember, I've wanted to be a great white, but I'm a hammerhead who *outwitted* a great white. It's not just G-White who has the shark factor.

I've got BUCKETS FULL of it!

HARRY

Species:

hammerhead shark

You'll spot him . . .

using his special

hammer-vision

Favorite thing:

his Gregor the Gnasher

poster

Most likely to say:

"I wish I was a great white."

Most embarrassing moment: when Mom called him

her "little starfish" in front of all his friends

RALPH

Species:
pilot fish

You'll spot him . . .
eating the food from
between
Harry's teeth!

Favorite thing: shrimp Pop-Tarts

Most likely to say: "So, Harry, what's for
breakfast today?"

Most embarrassing moment: eating too much cake
on Joe's birthday. His face was COVERED in pink
plankton icing.

JOE

Species: jellyfish

You'll spot him . . . hiding behind Ralph and Harry, or behind his own tentacles

Favorite thing: his cave, since it's nice and safe

Most likely to say: "If we do this, we're going to end up as fish food. . . ."

Most embarrassing moment: whenever his rear goes *toot*, which is when he's scared. Which is all the time.

RICK

Species: blacktip reef shark

You'll spot him . . . bullying smaller fish or showing off

Favorite thing: his black leather jacket

Most likely to say: "Last one there's a sea snail!"

Most embarrassing moment: none. Rick's far too cool to get embarrassed.

SHARK BITES

The basking shark is the second-largest fish in existence. Only the whale shark is bigger. Their mouths can be more than three feet in width!

An electric eel does not have teeth. It can grow up to nine feet in length.

Starfish are also known as sea stars. Although most starfish have five arms, some can have as many as twelve!

Piranha are freshwater fish mostly found in the waters of South America. They are carnivorous, which means they eat meat.

Most great white sharks are between thirteen and sixteen feet long and weigh from 1,500 to 2,450 pounds.

The teeth of great white sharks are razor sharp.

Sea cows are also known as manatees. They can stay underwater for about fifteen minutes, but must breathe air from the surface in order to survive.

Sharks have been swimming in the world's oceans for over 400 million years.

There are more than four hundred different species of sharks, ranging from the giant hammerhead to the goblin shark.

Sharks do not have bones. They are cartilaginous fish, which means their skeletons are made of cartilage, not bone. Cartilage is a type of connective tissue that is softer than bone. Humans have cartilage in their ears and nose.

The shortfin mako is the fastest shark in the ocean. It can swim in bursts as fast as forty-six miles per hour.

The whale shark is the largest shark in the sea and can grow to be as long as sixty feet.

DAVY OCEAN has traveled the seven seas in search of good seafaring shanties and fishy tales. He currently resides in a small fishing town that overlooks Shark Point and allows him uninterrupted access to the antics of a small community of hammerhead sharks and its fellow ocean neighbors.

AARON BLECHA is an artist who designs funny characters, animates silly cartoons, and illustrates humorous books. His work incudes illustrations for the bestselling book series George Brown, Class Clown. Originally from the United States, Aaron now lives with his family by the south English seaside.